Little Boy Soup

Little Boy Soup

Hardcover ISBN 978-1-939454-54-6
Epub ISBN 978-1-939454-74-4
Kindle ISBN 978-1-939454-78-2
Library of Congress Control Number: 2016932707
Cataloging in Publication data pending.

Published in the United States by
Balcony 7 Media and Publishing
530 South Lake Avenue #434
Pasadena, CA 91101
www.balcony7.com

Cover and Interior Illustrations by Amalia Hillmann
Cover & Interior Design by 3 Dog Creative

Printed in the United States of America

Distributed to the trade by:
Ingram Publisher Services
Mackin
Overdrive
Baker & Taylor (through IPS)

Little Boy Soup

Joshua Russell

Illustrations by
Amalia Hillmann

BALCONY 7
media & publishing

Playing in dirt,
from my head to my toes

with my pail and my ball
and with Dad's garden hose.

I want to keep playing
but I have to go in.

I don't want to wash
all the dirt off my skin.

HOT WATER,
COLD BUBBLES,
and toys I can scrub;

they all come in with me,
into the tub.

Dad stirs the water,
I grab the scoop.

Now we can play
Little Boy Soup!

Some bots? YEAH, a few.

And my whole
zombee crew!

I stir them up good

while Dad adds
SHAMPOO!

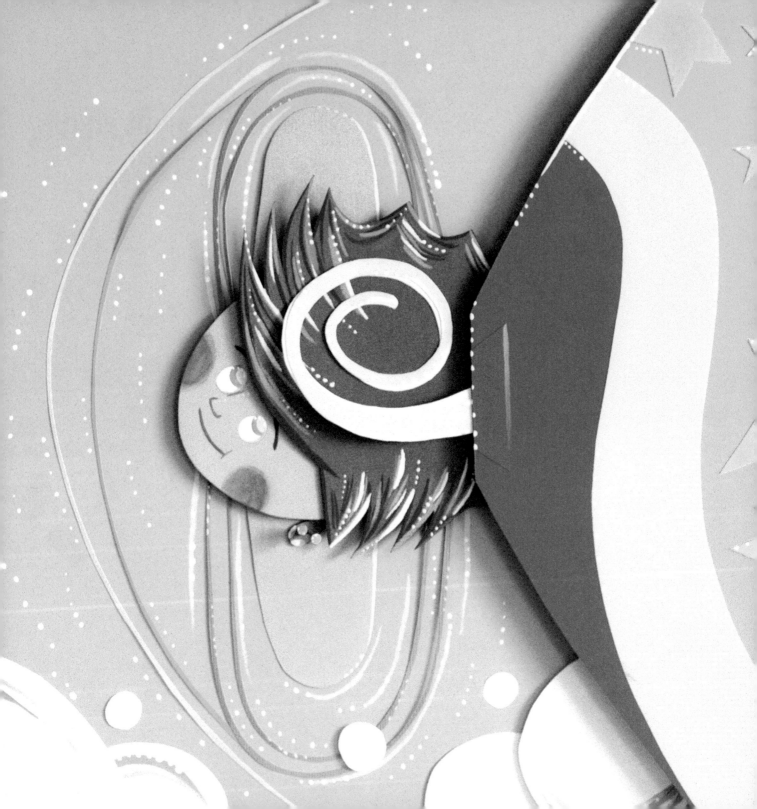

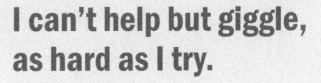

I can't help but giggle,
as hard as I try.

"Your belly's all smelly,
my stinky small fry."

"This water gun's loaded
so stick 'em up high!"

I put on my goggles
and reach for the sky!

I call in the troops.
They go on a tear!

**But the Ninjas
are faster!**

**They hide
in my hair.**

Before I forget,
and while I'm all wet,

I make Dad a list
of our best-est soup yet!

"Our soup is all done!
In a towel you go.

On to Course 2,
Little Boy Burrito!"

THE END

Learn more about the authors >

Coming Next
Little Girl Tea

ABOUT THE AUTHOR:

Joshua Russell is passionate about social responsibility in Silicon Valley, where his focus is on ensuring a strong presence of arts and creativity for children and adults. He is proactive in local philanthropy, encouraging community engagement via donations and volunteerism. His contribution to the community also includes leadership in organizations such as the San Jose Public Library Foundation. Russell is a graduate of the University of Arizona.

ABOUT THE ILLUSTRATOR:

Amalia Hillmann earned a Bachelor of Fine Arts in Graphic Design and Illustration from Concordia University, Nebraska. She returned to her Silicon Valley roots as a full-time artist, innovating through a variety of mediums and art forms for numerous creative endeavors, including illustrations and designs for sale on Etsy.com and her uniquely layered techniques for illustrating contemporary picture books.

ABOUT THE ILLUSTRATIONS:

Each illustration in *Little Boy Soup* is brought to life through layers of colorful paper carefully cut and arranged on illustration board. Amalia Hillmann sketches and designs each spread by hand, then crafts the final image with cardstock and paper. Final touches are added in gouache paint and then the designs are ready for you to enjoy.

CPSIA information can be obtained at www.ICGtesting.com
Printed in the USA
BVOW05*1425140816

458994BV00019B/74/P